# ChuckBone Battle Of The Monsters

Barry J McDonald

# Chapter 1

SparkleGirl lit her torch and held it above her head. Thankfully the way ahead looked clear of any hostile mobs. Working her way deeper into the cave SparkleGirl paused when she heard a sound coming from up ahead. Although hard to work out at first, there was no mistaking what it was saying. "You're a monster, you're a monster, you're a monster." SparkleGirl stared into the darkness ahead but couldn't see the source of the sound. "Who's there?" she called out. "Show yourself, or are you too scared to come out and face me." Taking no chances she pulled out her sword and continued walking on.

"SparkleGirl's a monster, SparkleGirl's a monster," the mysterious voice now repeated. "Come out of your hiding place and show yourself," SparkleGirl roared into the blackness. "Let me see the person who's calling me a monster." "You'll see, oh you'll see, follow me follow me," the voice whispered back. For the first time since she'd heard the voice it now seemed to be giving its location away. It seemed to be somewhere directly in front of her.

Gripping her sword tightly and holding her torch high to light the way, SparkleGirl ran in the direction of the voice. "The monsters coming, the monsters coming, the monsters coming." "I'll show you who's a monster when I find you," SparkleGirl called out as she ran. "Yes you will, yes you will," the voice teased repeating itself.

The more the voice spoke, the faster SparkleGirl found herself running towards it. "Stop, you fool," SparkleGirl said to herself. What an idiot she'd been running blindly into a cave on the hunt for an enemy she couldn't see. "SparkleGirl you idiot, who knows what's up ahead. You could be running into a pit, a group of hostile mobs or something worse. Give it up and go back." Realizing what a fool she'd been, SparkleGirl retraced her steps back to where she had started.

"You're nearly there, you're nearly there," the voice whispered from in front of her now. What the hell, SparkleGirl thought to herself. How could this person suddenly be in front of her? She hadn't seen or heard anyone go past her. Must be my imagination, SparkleGirl thought to herself. She'd been under a lot of stress lately and maybe this was her mind playing tricks on her. But it wasn't. Whatever could be said for hearing things, she was now also seeing things. Back at the place where she'd begun the chase, she now found a full length mirror waiting for her.

"What the…" SparkleGirl turned and looked all around her. How could a mirror suddenly appear out of nowhere? Minecraft could be a strange place at times but even this was going too far. Putting her sword away SparkleGirl moved closer to the mirror. While she wouldn't call herself a vain type of person she still felt compelled to look into the mirror. "That's it, that's it," the mysterious voice whispered as she walked forward. Although she'd fought the attempts by the voice to control her actions earlier, this time it was different. She felt compelled to see what was in the mirror. Now standing in front of the mirror SparkleGirl screamed at what she saw.

Looking at what was reflected back at her, SparkleGirl couldn't take her eyes off the image. "You're a monster, you're a monster, you're a monster, you're a monster," the voice screamed out with joy. "No. It can't be, no, no," SparkleGirl cried out and touched her face. Standing looking back at her was a reflection she didn't recognise. Her face wasn't her own anymore but was Herobrine's with his bright burning eyes. Then there were her hands. Looking at her hands in the reflection SparkleGirl recoiled at what she saw. They were both covered in blood that was dripping to the ground. "No. That's not me, that's not me," SparkleGirl repeated to herself and touched her face all over to prove it. "Oh, but that is you," a voice spoke up from behind her.

SparkleGirl spun around and found herself face to face with ChuckBone. "You!" SparkleGirl said and pulled out her sword. "I said you were a monster and now you've even seen it for yourself. Look at the blood on those hands," ChuckBone said and looked downward. Following ChuckBone's eyes SparkleGirl looked down and gazed at her sword hand. Like the image in the mirror, her hand in real life was also drenched in blood. "Arrrgh!" SparkleGirl screamed at what she now saw. "You're a monster too SparkleGirl. But you just won't admit it," ChuckBone said with a sneer and then started to laugh.

"I'm not a monster, I'm not a monster, I'm not a monster," SparkleGirl kept repeating to herself.

# Chapter 2

"Wake up, wake up," Emman said shaking SparkleGirl awake. "I'm not a... what, where am I?" SparkleGirl asked sitting up and looking around her. "It's me Emman. You were having a nightmare. I could see you were having a rough time, so I woke you up. You kept repeating something about being a monster or something. Are you OK?" Emman asked. "Yeah fine, it was nothing. Just a dream," SparkleGirl answered feeling embarrassed.

"So what's happening down below?" SparkleGirl asked climbing out of their temporary shelter. "Not much by the looks of it. Looks like you were right SparkleGirl, they've been chopping down every tree in sight," Emman said lying down beside her. "I knew ChuckBone wouldn't want to swim across. He'd rather be the big man leading a fleet of boats over to Herobrine's island," SparkleGirl said and ducked her head down. "It's not just that," Emman said. "It looks like he's waiting for other players to join up with him. I've been watching while you've been asleep and he's been sending players out in all directions. When they return they each bring a group of players back with them. Sometimes five, maybe ten, the biggest I saw was twenty. He really means business this time."

SparkleGirl thought over what Emman had said. She knew it's wasn't ChuckBone's magnetic charm that was drawing these players to him. It was the chance to kill Herobrine that everyone was interested in. "If I'm being honest here SparkleGirl, I think this is a suicide mission we're going on. How are we ever going to get near ChuckBone to stop him? And that's not taking into account the fact that it seems that he can't be killed. I'm your friend and everything, but maybe this is too much even for you," Emman said looking at SparkleGirl.

SparkleGirl had to agree, Emman had a point. The odds looked massively stacked against them. But did that mean they should just sit back and let ChuckBone have free rein to do whatever he wanted. Whatever those players down there had been promised, she knew that ChuckBone would go back on his deals once all of this was over. Whether those players knew it or not, Herobrine was their only hope. Yes, he may have done some bad things in the past but that was because his mind had been twisted that way. But ChuckBone, he had an evil streak in him from the very beginning and it was only getting worse. He had to be stopped.

"I agree with you Emman, it doesn't look good. In fact the odds of us winning this battle probably has a lot of zeroes on one side followed by a very small number at the other end. I can understand if you want to go now, in fact maybe you should. You don't have to come with me on this. This is a fight I'm a part of and I need to be there at the end, no matter what happens. I know we're friends and all, but even this is asking too much of you. Why not pack up your things and head back to my home, you can have it if you want to Emman," SparkleGirl added. "That sounds like a great offer but I'll have to pass on it, nice house and all that it is. I need to be here. I know I'm not the best but whatever help I can give you it's yours," Emman said and smiled. "And anyway, maybe I'll become a part of Minecraft history in the process." SparkleGirl laughed when she heard that. "Maybe Emman, and then again, maybe we might go down as the two biggest idiots in Minecraft." At this they both broke out into fits of laughter.

As the laughing died down, SparkleGirl thought over what they'd need to do. Thankfully the expanse of sea was delaying ChuckBone for a while. Which could give her more time to come up with a plan. "So what can we do, other than run around and set fire to every tree in Minecraft?" Emman said jokingly. "Set fire… set fire? Emman you're a genius," SparkleGirl said and slapped him on the shoulder. "I'm a what, how? So we go around burning trees, I was only joking!" Emman remarked.

"No. Not the trees, the boats. We're going to burn all the boats!" SparkleGirl said and broke out in a wide grin. "Now hold on a minute. You think we're going to be able to go down there, set fire to all the boats under ChuckBone's nose, and just walk away. You're crazy," Emman said not believing what he'd heard. "Yup, and do you know what's even better. We're going to take two boats for ourselves at the same time," SparkleGirl said her grin getting larger. Emman looked back in disbelief. Whatever you could say about SparkleGirl Emman thought, you had to give it to her, she was either incredibly brave or totally insane.

"So what do you think? Is that a great plan or what," SparkleGirl said feeling more confident. "I think we'll have this battle won even before it begins." Emman smiled back not feeling confident at all. "Maybe you should have taken me up on that offer of a free house," SparkleGirl said seeing the expression on Emman's face. "So when do we do this?" Emman asked. "I'd say about now" SparkleGirl said climbing out of the shelter and running off. "Is she always like this Wolfie2?" Emman asked looking at SparkleGirl's dog. Wolfie2 snorted back as if to agree with Emman and then he too ran off after SparkleGirl. "Aw well, here goes nothing," Emman said and wondered if this wasn't the craziest thing he'd ever done.

# Chapter 3

The closer Emman got to the campsite, the more he was regretting his decision to stay. "Psst over here, behind you," SparkleGirl called out. "Where were you going Emman? You walked right by me there. I thought you were going to do it all on your own," SparkleGirl whispered and started to giggle. "Very funny," Emman replied. "It's pitch black now, how was I supposed to see where you went. I thought you'd already gone on without me. So what's the plan?"

"I wish there was a plan Emman. But we're just going to have to play this one by ear. Once we get down there, I'm going to need some flint and steel," SparkleGirl said. "And you mister, you're not coming with us. I'll be back in a while to fetch you. So for now you're staying here. You hear me Wolfie2? You'll only draw attention to us and we really don't need that right now. OK Emman, are you ready to go?" Before Emman had a chance to answer SparkleGirl, she was up and gone. "God, I hate it when she does that," Emman swore and ran after her.

"Are we just going to walk into camp?" Emman asked after he'd caught up with SparkleGirl. "Yup." "But that's crazy we'll be spotted. Wouldn't it just be better to sneak into camp," Emman asked. "If we're caught sneaking in it'll look obvious that we're up to no good Emman. And you said it yourself, there's new players joining this group all the time. So what's two more players going to make any difference?" SparkleGirl replied. Emman knew SparkleGirl was probably right, but that thought still didn't do anything to slow down his wildly racing heart and the cold sweat that was forming on his back. "OK, here we go," SparkleGirl whispered as they walked from the complete darkness of night into the light from the torches that surrounded the camp.

"If only this were the real world," SparkleGirl whispered and pointed to the ring of torches that surrounded the camp. "Yeah if only, one torch in the wrong place and this whole place with go up in flames," Emman said with a smile. "Stop there. Who are you?" a voice called out from behind them. "Who us," SparkleGirl asked turning around to face the player. "We're here for the big battle. I hear ChuckBone's found out where Herobrine is and we're here to join the fun. That guy messed up our village last year, killed almost everyone except me and my brother here. Now's our chance to see the great Herobrine get sorted once and for all."

"Good, we could use as many players as possible. You two go over to the other side of camp and find FinnSolo. He'll show you what we need you to do," the player said and pointed the way. "Thanks so much. Oh by the way, where's ChuckBone? We've heard a lot about him but never met him. Any chance we could drop by and say hello?" SparkleGirl asked and started to play coyly with the end of her hair. "Ahem… not much chance of that. You see that large shelter over there. He's in there right now working out a battle plan for beating Herobrine," the player said now looking uncomfortable. "Ah well maybe another time. You take care now," SparkleGirl said and started to flutter her eyelids at the now blushing player. "Ahem… FinnSolo, yeah FinnSolo, that's who you're looking for. I better be off," the player said and quickly walked away as fast as he could.

"You enjoyed all of that didn't you? You take care now. Oh you big brave player you. That guy couldn't wait to get out of here," Emman said giving SparkleGirl a dig in the ribs with his elbow. "It works every time! I knew he'd get so embarrassed he'd be in a hurry to get away from us. And what about that guy, FinnSolo, what a name. I wonder if he has a Wookie with him," SparkleGirl said and started to laugh. "Come on Emman we need to get our hands on an enchanting table."

Walking through the large camp site SparkleGirl and Emman tried their best not to draw any attention to themselves. While they knew ChuckBone's location they couldn't be sure they wouldn't bump into any of his close friends who might know their identity. As they moved along SparkleGirl and Emman couldn't help but be impressed by how well ChuckBone had everything organized. Coming into camp, player after player emerged from the darkness with their inventory filled with wood which they dumped on the ground. This was taken up by other players who worked the raw wood into planks, which were then placed on the ground. Those planks were then worked on by more players who transformed the planks into sticks for the boat builders. "Wow, whatever you think of ChuckBone he really knows how to organize an assembly line. He must have… just a rough guess, but there must be a hundred boats here, and enough planks for a hundred more," Emman said turning to SparkleGirl. "That's what has me worried Emman, it's too well organized. I never would have thought ChuckBone had the brain power to do all of this. This just proves to me how much we really need to stop him. He can't be allowed to take all those players across the water to Herobrine. Come on let's find that enchanting table," SparkleGirl said leading the way.

After a short walk to the other side of the camp, SparkleGirl and Emman stumbled across ChuckBone's second assembly line. They both marvelled as they watched almost twenty players hard at work on crafting and enchanting tables, producing everything from arrows to armour. "He really wants to win this fight," Emman said looking at the piles of weaponry on the ground. "How can we ever beat all of this?" SparkleGirl looked at the scene in front of her and had to agree, they now looked massively outnumbered and out-gunned.

# Chapter 4

"I know it looks bad Emman, much worse than I thought it would be. But I've got to do something about all of this. I can't let ChuckBone kill Herobrine and take over Minecraft. You know how that would turn out if he did," SparkleGirl said. "You said it again!" Emman said. "You said you'd have to do something, not we, you. Don't forget you've got me by your side now. So the chances of you succeeding here probably have gone up two percent!" "You're such a clown Emman, you know that," SparkleGirl said laughing. "But seriously I'm glad you're here with me. I wouldn't be able to do this without you. Come on, let's take ChuckBone down."

Working their way over to the enchanting tables SparkleGirl stopped and laughed. "I think I've just spotted FinnSolo, Emman. At the end there, at the last enchanting table." "Where?" Emman asked scanning the faces. "Oh yeah, that wasn't too hard to work out." Standing at the last table Emman spotted two players, one wearing a Chewbacca skin and the other one trying to look like Han Solo. "OK Emman just follow my lead and please, let me do the talking," SparkleGirl said and started walking in the direction of the two players.

"FinnSolo I presume?" SparkleGirl asked walking up to the player. "How did you know that?" the player replied looking confused. "Oh, just a lucky guess I suppose," SparkleGirl said and grinned. "We were sent over here by another player who said you might have some work for us. We wanted to join in the attack against Herobrine, me and my brother here. So where do we start?" "I take it you can work a crafting table," FinnSolo asked SparkleGirl. "Yeah sure, anything you need. You just give me the ingredients and I'll do the rest," SparkleGirl replied confidently. "And what about your brother there," Chewbacca asked. "Oh him, he's a cluts. You're safer keeping him away from one. The last time he worked on a crafting table he blew his eyebrows off. I didn't think it was possible until I saw it for myself. Nah, he can just stand there and watch me. Safer for all of us if you ask me Chewy," SparkleGirl said with a grin.

"Yeah, probably right," FinnSolo remarked, "So can you make arrows? As you can see ChuckBone wants to be well equipped before we meet

Herobrine and God only know what he has on that island." "But we won't have to worry about those hostile mobs after Herobrine's dead," Chewbacca remarked. "How so?" Emman asked. "Because they'll be all dead" "No, did you not hear? Once ChuckBone kills Herobrine he's going to take his power from him. Then he'll be able to control all the hostile mobs in Minecraft. Cool, huh," Chewbacca said with a grin. SparkleGirl looked at Emman and she could tell he was having the same thought as her. This wasn't a simple revenge attack for what Herobrine had done to him. This battle was so much more. ChuckBone wanted to become the ultimate player in Minecraft and these idiots couldn't see that. This was worse than she thought.

"We'll leave you two here to get on with your work," FinnSolo said and then leaned in close to SparkleGirl and whispered. "And by the way keep your brother away from that table. The last thing I need is something going wrong and me getting the blame for it." "Sure, no problem. ChuckBone will love our work, you can count on that," SparkleGirl whispered back with a smile.

Emman waited until the two players had walked away and went over to SparkleGirl. "So I'm the idiot brother am I," Emman said his feelings now hurt. "You should have seen the look on your face Emman, it was priceless. But seriously I didn't know how much you knew about crafting tables. I had to make up some excuse to keep you away from it. It worked, didn't it," SparkleGirl said with a smile. "OK, it worked," Emman said begrudgingly. "And anyway that's not important right now," SparkleGirl said. "You heard what he said, ChuckBone wants Herobrine's power over the hostile mobs. This is worse they we thought. Even if we stop him this time, he's just going to keep coming back again and again until he kills Herobrine. No, we're going to have to find a way to stop him permanently."

"But how?" Emman asked. "He's indestructible now. There's no way we can beat that." "I know Emman. I don't know what we're going to do, but we'll come up with something, I hope. Let's just stick to the plan for now," SparkleGirl said and took flint and steel out of her inventory and added them to the crafting table. "Emman while you're here, maybe it's best if I share some of my inventory with you. The last thing you need is me getting

11

killed and you're left defenceless," SparkleGirl said and started putting all her items on the ground. "Wow, where did you get all that stuff from? Potions, ender pearls and TNT. I didn't realize you were packing so much heat," Emman chuckled and picked up what he might need. "Well a girl has to be prepared Emman. Who knows what she might need when the occasion arises. And anyway it's not all mine, I picked up most of that stuff back at ChuckBone's fort. Now hurry up before someone sees all of those weapons!"

After he had finished, Emman watched SparkleGirl worked the flint and steel together. "How long is this going to take? It won't be long before those two Star Wars fans come back to see how we're getting on," Emman asked looking around him nervously. "Take a chill pill Emman I'm nearly there. I've created enough flint and steel to burn this place down twice over. When those boats go up in flames I don't want ChuckBone having any chance of putting them out. Right, I'm finished," SparkleGirl said and turned around.

Leaving the crafting table area SparkleGirl and Emman walked over to the large group of boats that were sitting on the beach. "OK we'd better be quick before we're noticed. Emman grab those two boats there and pull them far from here. The last thing we need right now is our escape plan going up in flames too. When you've done that, go get Wolfie2 and bring him back here. And don't take long Emman, once I start lighting these boats we won't have much time. Now off you go," SparkleGirl said checking that no one was watching them.

After watching Emman walk away with their two boats, SparkleGirl turned her attention back to the job at hand, burning everything in sight.

# Chapter 5

"Wolfie2 where are you?" Emman called out into the darkness. "Darn it dog, we don't have time for this," Emman swore and called out again. Standing from his vantage point up high on the hill, Emman turned back to look at the activity that was going on below him and wondered how SparkleGirl was getting on. "Wolfie2 come on. We don't have time for this, believe me!" Emman said turning his attention back to finding Wolfie2. "Is this your dog? He's nice," a voice spoke. "Now throw down your weapons!"

Before Emman could say or do anything the darkness was lit up by a torch. Standing in front of him Emman found himself facing two players who looked anything but friendly. "We've been watching you, what are you doing around here?" the first player asked. "We... I mean... I, I'm here to help with the battle," Emman said hoping the player didn't noticed his mistake. "You said we, who's we?" the player asked. "Erm, me and the dog there," Emman said pointing to Wolfie2 who was now being held on a lead. "Oh, I don't think so. We watched you leaving the camp, it was obvious you were up to no good. Now out with it. Who are you with, where did you come from, and what are you really doing here?" the player asked moving forward menacingly.

Emman wondered what SparkleGirl would do in this situation. She'd probably play along and then cut the two players down when they were least expecting it. But that was SparkleGirl. He on the other hand, wasn't so confident that he'd be able to take on these two players and walk away unharmed. But this was one battle he had to win, lose it and all their plans and chance of success would be gone in an instant. What would SparkleGirl do? Emman wondered to himself. Then looking through his inventory and remembering an old story SparkleGirl had told him, he came up with an idea.

Holding an ender pearl in his hand, Emman flicked it towards the two players. "Ouch, what the hell was that?" the first player asked holding his hand up to his eye. "He threw something at me?" In what seemed like a lifetime but was in fact only a second or two, Emman watched the confusion on the second players face before ender pearl hit the ground. Once it touched down, Emman was instantly teleported to where the first player was standing. The only problem was he was still unarmed.

"What the..." the player cried out in amazement as he found himself looking straight into Emman's face. Using the confusion Emman realized that even though he was unarmed he still had a chance to win this fight. Pushing off the ground as hard as he could, Emman used the top of his head as a battering ram and launched himself into the players face. He knew the instant his head connected with the players chin, there was no way the player was going to be getting up again.

Looking down at the unconscious player at his feet, Emman smiled to himself. Wow, SparkleGirl would have been proud of that, he thought before he was interrupted by a voice from behind him. "I'd like to see you try that with me," the second player said. Emman turned around to find the second player now looking even angrier than before. "What a coward using ender pearls in a fight. I'd like to see you try that again," the player said and moved forward with his sword drawn. Looking at the player Emman could see he wouldn't be getting out of this confrontation as easily as the first one. Pulling his sword out and making sure he had a good grip of it, Emman stepped forward to fight. With all his attention on the oncoming player, Emman completely forgot about Wolfie2 until Wolfie2 made his presence known. Jumping in from the side Wolfie2 gripped the player's sword arm tightly and fought with it until his sword dropped to the ground.

"Aaarrggh, get that mutt off me," the player screamed rolling around on the ground with Wolfie2 on top of him. "You can let him go now boy, he's not going to cause us any more problems," Emman said and pulled on Wolfie2's collar. Emman looked at the player on the ground and his mangled arm and felt sorry for him. "Sorry about that, it was nothing personal but there's something I need to do," Emman said pulling Wolfie2 back off the player. "Whatever it is, you won't get away with it," the player said with a grin, "You're going to have so many players after you, you'll wish you never met me." Now confused Emman didn't see the player pull out a dagger until it was too late. Gripping it in his hands the player stabbed himself hard in the stomach. "When I respawn back at camp, I'll be coming back up here with an army to get yoooo...." the second player said before passing away. Emman stood in shock as the players body faded away and disappeared. Then he looked back down to the campsite below. "Oh God, run Wolfie2," Emman roared and took off running as fast as he could downhill.

# Chapter 6

It didn't take long before SparkleGirl heard the commotion in the camp and realized they'd been rumbled. "We're being attacked," a player screamed running out of a shelter. "Up on the hill. Quick, follow me." SparkleGirl watched as the player gathered a handful of players to him and started running out of camp. "Oh Emman, all you had to do was go get the dog," SparkleGirl sighed to herself. Moving as quickly as she could, SparkleGirl ran from boat to boat and touched her flint and steel on as many of them as she could. Now that Emman had been spotted she knew it would only be a matter of time before they came across her as well. "Come on, come on," SparkleGirl said to herself trying in some way to speed herself up. Then she heard a shocked voice call out from behind her.

"What the hell are you doing?" a player exclaimed seeing the first signs of fire coming from the first boats. Turning as quickly as she could SparkleGirl took out her bow and answered his question with an arrow in the chest. Forgetting the next few boats, SparkleGirl ran to the end boat and lit it. She knew she'd never get them all burned, but if she could make their salvage a lot harder to do, it would help make their getaway easier. Before leaving the beach SparkleGirl tossed two bundles of TNT into two boats that were just starting to catch fire and ran for her life.

Diving to the ground, SparkleGirl felt the heat of the blast pass over her back and move up the beach. "The boats are on fire, the boats are on fire," a player screamed running towards her. "What happened?" he asked helping SparkleGirl to her feet. "Five players, I don't know who they were, started setting fire to the boats. I tried to stop them but I got caught in the explosion. They ran that way," SparkleGirl said and pointed in the opposite direction.

Once everyone in the camp had heard the explosion, it didn't take long before more and more players came running to the scene. SparkleGirl knew she wouldn't have much more time. Moving as quickly as she could and without drawing attention to herself, she moved further up the beach towards one of the camps shelters. Then crouching in the shadow of the building she watched the scene unfold and grinned when she saw

ChuckBone approaching.

"What happened here?" ChuckBone screamed out in anger. "Wasn't anyone guarding the boats?" SparkleGirl watched as the player she'd encountered on the beach ran over. "ChuckBone, there were five players, they set fire to the boats and ran off. We're hunting them down right now," the player said. "Five players, who were they, who saw them?" ChuckBone screamed into the players face. "It was a player, she was here a moment ago," the player remarked scanning the surrounding faces. "She's gone now. But she's the one who told me what had happened." "What did she look like, this girl? Did she have long red hair?" SparkleGirl watched as the player nervously nodded his head up and down before being punched in the face by ChuckBone. "Idiot!" ChuckBone roared. "That was SparkleGirl you let escape. I don't know how she did it, but that's the last she'll get away from me. Pull this place apart and look for her!"

"He looks really annoyed," a voice spoke from behind SparkleGirl. Turning around with her sword drawn she found Emman and Wolfie2 beside her. "Oh thank God. I thought I was going to have to go out there and look for you. But wait, how did you get past those players that went running out of camp?" SparkleGirl remarked. "Well that was all thanks to you. Once they heard that explosion of yours they quickly changed their minds. Then all I had to do was follow behind them into camp. Then thanks to Wolfie2 here, he sniffed you out and well, here we are," Emman said with a grin. "It's so good to see you Emman, but let's get out of here. I'd hate for ChuckBone to catch us after all of this. Come on, let's go."

Moving through the shadows SparkleGirl, Emman and Wolfie2 made their way to their boats. Further up the beach they could see ChuckBone's players fighting the flames of the last remaining boats without much success. "Wolfie2 you go with Emman. Don't worry it's just for now. I'll meet up with you both soon," SparkleGirl said and gave her dog a hug. "Emman you and Wolfie2 go first. I'll stay here just to make sure you get away OK." Helping them into the boat and giving it a push off, SparkleGirl watched as Emman and Wolfie2 floated out to sea unnoticed by anyone on the beach.

"Right, here we go!" SparkleGirl said and climbed into her boat. Using her bow to push herself away, she turned and kept it trained on the beach behind her. Thankfully it looked like she too had gotten away without being noticed. But then she passed from the cover of darkness and floated within the glow of the burning boats. "Hey, there's someone out there," a player called out pointing in her direction. "Over there in a boat." Helpless to do anything SparkleGirl watched as the player ran towards the rest of the group and pointed to what he'd seen. "Damn you big mouth," SparkleGirl swore to herself.

"It's SparkleGirl, get her!" ChuckBone screamed to the players that surrounded him. "The one that kills her gets as many diamond's as they can carry. Get her!" Watching the crowd of players getting ready on the beach, SparkleGirl knew she was in trouble. Then just as she feared would happen, the first arrow came out in the night's sky and splashed down close to her boat. Then like a swarm of whistling hornet's the rest followed.

# Chapter 7

Apart from the fact that he really wanted her dead, SparkleGirl knew why ChuckBone had wanted her killed right now. Without a boat he wasn't able to get his hands on her but if she died out here, he knew she'd have to respawn back on dry land. Then he could have his revenge.

SparkleGirl curled up into a ball in the bottom of the boat and tried to make her body as small as possible. Thankfully the first wave of arrows splashed down in the sea with only a few arrows hitting her boat, but she knew that would change. As players readjusted their sights and took another shot, it would only be a matter of time before someone got lucky. She might survive a few direct hits from an ordinary bow but if an arrow came from an enchanted one, well, it wasn't worth thinking about. Reaching into her inventory SparkleGirl retrieved a health potion and held it in her hand. "Let's hope I don't have to use you," she said to the small bottle and curled up tightly again.

For the first time in Minecraft SparkleGirl found herself very afraid. She'd been in situations before that were as frightening as this, but she always had the ability to fire back at her enemies. This time she couldn't and it was this lack of power that scared her. Listening to the arrow bolts thumping into the woodwork of the boat made SparkleGirl want to scream. But she couldn't let that happen. The last thing she wanted right now was for ChuckBone to know how scared she was. Then without warning, SparkleGirl's leg erupted in terrible pain.

"Aaarrgh!" SparkleGirl screamed out and looked down to where the pain was coming from. There standing proudly was the shaft of an arrow. While the pain was intense right now,

SparkleGirl could tell the arrow had thankfully only come from an ordinary bow. Grabbing the shaft of the arrow, she grit her teeth and pulled it free. "Damn you ChuckBone!" SparkleGirl swore to the arrow before throwing it over the side of the boat. Then her shoulder exploded in pain. SparkleGirl screamed out in agony. It now looked like ChuckBone was going to get his wish. It would only take another arrow or two and then it would be game over.

Pulling the top off her health potion and spitting it away, SparkleGirl swallowed the full measure in one gulp. Instantly she could feel the power and energy traveling to every area of her body. Now that she felt stronger, she felt better up to the task of pulling the arrow free of her shoulder. SparkleGirl grimaced in pain as the bolt come slowly out of the wound and then watched as the hole closed over. She knew there was only one way she was going to survive this. "You're not going to beat me this time ChuckBone," SparkleGirl swore and then holding the side of the boat, she threw herself overboard.

Hitting the water SparkleGirl was relieved that she had made the decision when she had. Without warning another wave of arrows came out of the dark night sky and hit her boat over and over again. Holding onto the side of the boat that was facing away from the beach, SparkleGirl used it to as a barrier between herself and the archers. If Emman could see me now, SparkleGirl thought. Inside she was relieved that it was her in this situation and not Emman. Could he have coped with this, she wondered. The thought of Emman being killed and ending up in ChuckBone's hands wasn't worth thinking about. Holding tightly to the boat SparkleGirl was relieved when the number of arrows reaching her boat became fewer and fewer. It was looking like the tide was pulling her away from ChuckBone's grasp. Now she had the tough task of trying to get back into the boat again without sinking it.

Moving herself to the back of the boat, SparkleGirl grit her teeth and pulled her body up and out of the water. In what seemed like a fight that went on forever, she eventually broke free of the grip of the water and fell into the boat. Lying there she finally found herself beginning to relax. She knew this moment would pass once she reached the shore of Herobrine's island, but for now she felt better than she had in a long time. Watching the first clouds of morning float aimlessly across the sky, she found herself daydreaming without a care. Then she heard a familiar voice that brought her back to the real world. "Got room for two more?"

SparkleGirl sat up straight away when she heard the voice. "Emman is that...where are you?" Looking to the left and right, SparkleGirl eventually caught sight of Wolfie2 and Emman bobbing up and down in the sea.

"Going my way?" Emman asked with a chuckle. "Which way would that be?" SparkleGirl said in a serious voice. "Erm, we're going that way," Emman said pointing off to the horizon. "I've got to get to an island. Meet Herobrine. Start a war and all that. Want to come along?" "Sure, why not. It gets boring just floating around here out at sea," SparkleGirl said with a chuckle and paddled her boat over to her two friends.

# Chapter 8

"So what happened to you?" SparkleGirl asked after she had pulled Emman and Wolfie2 to the side of her boat. "Squid," Emman said with an embarrassed look on his face. "What do you mean, squid?" SparkleGirl asked puzzled. "Well how do I say it? I wasn't watching where I was going and never noticed a squid right in front of me. The last thing I knew Wolfie2 let out a bark, the boat smashed into it, and I was thrown overboard."

"Oh Emman, trust you to find a lone squid in all of this," SparkleGirl said with a giggle and pointed to the huge expanse of water. "It's alright for you, you're not the one bobbing up and down in the sea. This looks and feels ridiculous. I wish Notch would update Minecraft and gave me us the ability to swim properly because this looks daft," Emman grumbled. "Oh I don't know, you look cute bobbing up and down like that," SparkleGirl said and pushed down a little on Emman's head. "Bob."

"You do that one more time and you'll be fighting ChuckBone on your own!" Emman said bobbing back up after she'd lifted her hand off his head. "Sorry Bob, I won't do it again, Bob!" SparkleGirl said with a chuckle. "Enough, we've got a serious battle to fight and you're laughing at me bobbing up and down in the sea," Emman remarked getting annoyed. "Sorry, you're right Emman. I had a bad time back there and I'm so relieved to see you. Sorry I just got into a giddy mood. But in case I haven't already said it, it's great to see you, and you!" SparkleGirl said and gave Wolfie2 a tickle under the chin.

"So what's the plan?" Emman asked. "What do we do now, and are we even going in the right direction?" Standing up in the boat to see better, SparkleGirl searched the horizon for any sign of land. For a while it seemed like there was nothing out there, but then as the sun rose higher in the sky SparkleGirl could make out a mountain off to their right. "Over there, I see it, over there!" SparkleGirl said excitedly pointing in its direction. "Are we far away?" Emman asked. "Please say we're close." "Sorry Emman but it's going to take awhile to get there, hopefully we'll make it there before dark. The last thing I want is to be out here in the darkness with ChuckBone on our tail." "That's another thing, I wonder how he's getting on now that we've ruined his boats?" Emman asked with a grin. "From the last I saw of him he's not our biggest fan right now. I think it's best if we keep well out of his way until we meet Herobrine," SparkleGirl said. "Yeah Herobrine. He'll know what to do!" Emman said. "He'll kick ChuckBone's butt!"

"That's another thing I'm not looking forward to. Meeting Herobrine," SparkleGirl said with a worried look on her face. "How's he going to react when we show up? Hi Herobrine, it's so good to see. I know it's been a long time, oh and by the way, you better get your ass in gear because there's about two hundred players on the way to kill you. Yeah you heard me right, two hundred and they'll probably be here tomorrow. What's that? You're not happy to see me now, and you want to chop me and Emman's heads off. Yeah, you're probably right. We're going to all die here and it's all my fault. That's how I imagine our first conversation with Herobrine will go. What do you think Emman?" "After what you've just said SparkleGirl. Maybe its better if we turn this boat around and go far from both of these two," Emman said now feeling worried. "Believe me it's crossed my mind too Emman. But this problem is because of us, so it's only right that we try to help. It mightn't be much but we can't walk away from this. No matter how tempting it is. Now Bob get bobbing, we have to make it to that island before dark."

*****

Landing on the shore of Herobrine's island SparkleGirl and Emman stood for a while and watched Wolfie2 excitedly running around. "I know how he feels, I was feeling sick those last few minutes out there bobbing around like a cork," Emman said with relief. "Why don't we head over to that hill over there and have a look around. The sun's starting to go down, and I'd like to see what this place looks like while we've still got some daylight," SparkleGirl said and lead the way up the beach.

On reaching the top and looking out to sea, SparkleGirl was relieved to see that there was no sign of ChuckBone on the horizon. "It looks like we're not going to see ChuckBone anytime tonight. But it won't be long, not after the mood I saw him in. He's going to be working his players twice as hard this time. If we get through tomorrow without seeing him, we'll be really lucky," SparkleGirl said shielding her eyes from the setting sun. "That's another thing you didn't tell me, what happened to you back there. I thought you'd be right behind me but there was no sign of you. What happened?" Emman asked. Rubbing the spot where she had been hit in the shoulder, SparkleGirl waved off Emman's question, "Not much to say other than it was close call. I didn't think I was going to make it. But come on, let's forget all about that and go find Herobrine. Wolfie2 do you think you can sniff him out?"

Watching Wolfie2 get to work, SparkleGirl and Emman followed closely behind and took in the sights of the island. "It's beautiful here," Emman remarked looking around him. "You'd never think this was the kind of place you'd find Herobrine? I mean, I always imagined him sitting in some throne room in the Nether with lava all around him. But not here, it's so beautiful." SparkleGirl stopped in her tracks and then pulled out her sword. "I think you might change your mind about that Emman after you see this. Now get out your sword!"

# Chapter 9

Turning around to where SparkleGirl was looking, Emman let out a sigh. "Aw come on guys, we're only here!" Emman said to the hostile mobs that were coming their way. "One thing you can say about Herobrine, he may be a nice guy, but boy does he keep bad company" SparkleGirl said and got ready for the attack.

Without saying another word SparkleGirl was off and running to meet the first creeper, which she easily cut in two. Then she quickly finished off three zombies before pausing to see how Emman was getting on. "That's my boy," SparkleGirl remarked as she watched Emman fight a zombie and take its head off its shoulders. After a few moments of dealing with the remaining two creepers SparkleGirl and Emman stood back to catch their breath.

"Well what did you think? Did you see that?" Emman asked excitedly. "Yes I did and I'm impressed. You've come a long way from fighting off mobs with a stick," SparkleGirl said with a smile. "You're never going to let me live that down, are you? It only happened twice," Emman grumbled, fighting a grin that was coming onto his face. "We won this battle Emman, but there's a lot more hostile mobs where they came from. Like I said, anywhere you find Herobrine there'll be tons of those things with him. That's our biggest problem. We have to get close to him without getting killed. Maybe it's best if we build a shelter and some beds for the night. The last thing we need right now is to get killed here and respawn back on the mainland. I think you've had your fair share of swimming for a while," SparkleGirl said with a smile. "You can say that again," Emman said looking around him for a suitable place to find shelter. "How about over there?" "Looks good to me Emman. You get digging and I'll stand guard over here," SparkleGirl said taking out her bow and a handful or arrows.

As SparkleGirl watched Emman work his way into the hillside with his pickaxe. She remarked at how far he'd come on in the short time they'd been together. Thinking back to the first time when she'd met him, she had thought him to be a lost cause. But now he had the makings of a great Minecraft player. Apart from that she had grown very close to him. Now after a long time of living alone she had someone she could call a friend.

"Wow, you should see this," Emman called out from inside the shelter. "What is it now?" SparkleGirl called back. "You've finally found your brain." "No seriously, if you're looking for Herobrine I think I've just found him," Emman remarked. Making sure they were still no hostile mobs around, SparkleGirl dropped her bow and ran to where Emman was. "See I told you, but you didn't believe me," Emman said pointing to the back wall of their shelter. "I was just digging away there when I found it." Pulling Wolfie2 back out of the way and commanding him to stay put, SparkleGirl walked to the back wall and looked through the hole Emman had created. "See I told you so, there's a huge cavern down there. Someone's been busy mining under this island. If you look down and over to the right, there's two tunnels that lead away. I bet Herobrine built all of this. He's not living on the island, he's living under it," Emman added with a grin. "Come here, wait until I show you this." Without warning, Emman used his pickaxe and dug away a block from beside where SparkleGirl was standing. "No!" SparkleGirl screamed but it was too late. As she watched the block vanish, the floor under her feet suddenly gave way and she fell into the darkness below.

"Owww! SparkleGirl cried out when she hit the ground. Lying on her back she looked up to where she had fallen from and saw Emman looking down from above. "Are you OK?" he called from above. At this moment in time she wasn't too sure herself. Lying motionless on the ground she waited for the first signs of pain to kick in. Then it came. Like a speeding bullet to her brain, her arm told her that it had seen better days and now wanted her full attention. "Ooowww! SparkleGirl howled and moved her good hand to feel for damage. Luckily her bad arm didn't seem broken, but it was heavily bruised. What I wouldn't give for a health potion right now, SparkleGirl remarked to herself.

"Are you OK?" SparkleGirl looked up to see Emman waving wildly down to her. "Yeah I'm fine. But you and I are going to have a little chat when I get back up there," SparkleGirl called back. "I'm sorry, you hear me. I'm sorry," Emman shouted back down to her. "You will be when I get back up to you," SparkleGirl yelled back. "Oh God no. SparkleGirl watch out!" Turning to where Emman was pointing, SparkleGirl could see saw a glint of green coming towards her. Creepers.

Getting to her feet as quickly as she could, SparkleGirl watched as three creepers stepped out of the shadows and into the shaft of light that was coming from the hole far above her. By the way they were hissing, SparkleGirl knew she wouldn't have much time before they exploded. Reaching for her sword, she let out a howl of pain. Her sword arm, she'd totally forgotten about it. There was no way she could fight her way out of this. Moving backwards away from the group of creepers SparkleGirl stopped when her back came up against the cavern wall. She was out of time and no way to defend herself.

# Chapter 10

Emman watched from above and was helpless to do anything. Looking down on SparkleGirl he cringed as he watched her being surrounded. "I can't watch this," Emman cried to himself and closed his eyes tight. A second later the ground rocked below him from a huge explosion. Opening his eyes Emman raced to the opening in the back wall and looked down below. Looking to where SparkleGirl had been, he could see nothing but a large crater that the creepers had blown open. "Oh God I've killed her!" Emman sobbed looking at the mess below. Turning around and letting his body slump to the ground Emman turned to face Wolfie2. "I've done it, I've killed her. One of the best players in Minecraft and I've killed her. Killed by an idiot like me," Emman bawled out and started to cry.

Once his sadness had past, Emman's mind turned to rage as he thought about the situation that he now in. Looking out toward the world outside the cave, Emman cursed it all. "What am I doing here, I'm not even a good player. I wouldn't be here if it wasn't for her. Now that she's gone the whole of Minecraft is depending on me to stop ChuckBone. Me. What a joke. YOU HEAR ME, WHAT A JOKE!" Emman screamed. Now that he'd let it all out, Emman realized that he forgotten all about Wolfie2. Looking over at SparkleGirl's dog he tried his best to apologize to it. "You know I didn't mean it. I didn't mean to kill SparkleGirl and send her far away from here. You do know that, don't you?" Emman said wiping a tear away from his eye and giving Wolfie2 a hug. Looking at Emman, Wolfie2 gave a bark in response and then jumped to his feet. "You're right Wolfie2. Snap out of it, Emman," Emman said and slapped himself hard in the face. "Crying isn't going to bring her back. Like it or not, you're here and she's not. So what are you going to do about it?" Emman asked himself out loud. "Now what would SparkleGirl do?"

Looking around Emman realized he'd better close up both the entrance and the hole in the back wall. It mightn't be long before other hostile mobs came by and tried to finish him off too. What he needed right now was time to think and plan. Once morning came he'd know what to do, hopefully. After sealing everything up, Emman lit a torch and then made a bed for himself. Looking through his inventory Emman was grateful that SparkleGirl had the wisdom to share her things with him. Taking out some cooked pork chops he shared them with Wolfie2 and wondered what he should do next. Maybe his first move should be to visit the beach and see if there were any sign of ChuckBone. Then he'd know better how much time he had.

But then what? Should he go looking for Herobrine himself? And if he did, what would he say to him? "Oh hi Herobrine, you don't know me but I'm a good friend of SparkleGirl. Where is she? Oh I got her blown up by accident, but that's not important right now. There's another small thing you should know about. You remember ChuckBone, don't you? You won't believe this but he's on his way here. How does he know you're here? Oh, that's my fault too. What's that, you're going to chop my head off... I wouldn't blame you either," Emman groaned after playing the scenario over in his head. Turning to look at Wolfie2 Emman asked, "Is that how's it's going to play out. Herobrine killing me for being an idiot." Wolfie2 just yawned and closed his eyes to go to sleep. "Thanks. You're a great help," Emman said and got into bed. Maybe some sleep would help him to see things in a better light, he hoped.

*****

Waking the next morning Emman sat up and looked around him. "I guess yesterday wasn't a bad dream," Emman remarked realizing that SparkleGirl was still gone, "Oh well Wolfie2, let's see what trouble we can get ourselves in today." Punching his way through the front wall of his shelter, Emman covered his eyes against the bright daylight. "Come on boy, let's see how things look around here in the daytime." Taking Wolfie2 with him Emman knew his first stop would be to visit the high hill overlooking the beach. Scanning the horizon Emman was happy to see that there was no sign of ChuckBone on it. "Looks like it's taking ChuckBone a while to recover from our attack Wolfie2. But I can't see us getting any longer than another day without him showing his ugly face around here. If he doesn't come by tonight, he'll be here in the morning. Boy I wish SparkleGirl was here right now, she'd know what to do." Sitting down on the ground feeling dejected, Emman reached into his inventory and took out the last remaining pork chops and shared them with Wolfie2. "I guess it's all up to you and me now."

Looking out to sea again Emman sat in silence and wondered how SparkleGirl was getting on, back on the mainland.

# Chapter 11

Coughing from the dust of the explosion, SparkleGirl found herself lying on her back once more. "Twice in one day what are the odds," SparkleGirl remarked to herself. "A fall and now an explosion and that's even before we've met Herobrine. This is turning out to be one hell of a day!"

Taking her time getting to her feet, SparkleGirl allowed her body to give her a damage report on how it was doing. Thankfully the only body part that was still complaining was her sword arm. She'd been very lucky to survive the creeper attack. Once she'd seen the first creeper starting to flash she genuinely thought that it was all over. Thank goodness for cobwebs, SparkleGirl remarked. Grabbing a handful of cobwebs off the cave wall she'd thrown them at the approaching creepers and slowed down their countdown. It didn't buy her much time but that extra second or two had allowed her to throw herself behind a rock for cover.

Taking out and lighting up a torch, SparkleGirl took in the sight of the blast crater and then looked up to the hole above. Which was now gone. SparkleGirl stared in disbelief at the resealed wall and wondered if she'd been imagining things. That explosion might have given her shell shock, but she hadn't imagined falling down here. So where was it? Screaming at the top of her voice SparkleGirl called for Emman. "EMMAN CAN YOU HEAR ME? IT'S ME SPARKLEGIRL, EMMAN!" But there was no response. He must think I'm dead, SparkleGirl thought to herself, surely he'd know that if Wolfie2 was still on the island that I must be here as well. But then again, Emman had never had a dog of his own, so maybe he didn't know this.

Kicking herself for never telling him, SparkleGirl realized she was now on her own to find Herobrine. "Maybe it's best if I go the rest of the way without you Emman. I wouldn't want you getting hurt because of me. Stay safe and I'll see you later!" SparkleGirl said to wall above her. Then giving a wave farewell, SparkleGirl picked one of the tunnels that lead out of the cavern and followed it.

*****

"There's nothing else we can do," Emman said to Wolfie2. "Whether I like it or not, I'm going to have to find Herobrine and warn him. Not much of a plan is it." Wolfie2 snorted in response and looked away. "What else do you want me to do? God I wish SparkleGirl was here," Emman moaned and hid his face in his hands. "Come on Emman, you can do this. Forget about yourself for a change. This is for SparkleGirl," Emman said trying to motivate himself. "Aw who am I kidding? I'll be lucky if I get anywhere near Herobrine to tell him this!" Emman groaned and looked out to sea again. Then he saw something that left him with no choice. He'd need to find Herobrine.

On the horizon Emman could make out a handful of specks in the distance. There was no denying it now, ChuckBone was on his way. "That settles it, let's go boy!" Emman said jumping to his feet. "Like it or not, we've got to find Herobrine." Running to the nearest cave he could find, Emman paused long enough to light up a torch and take out his sword before running into it. Thinking as he ran, Emman thought back to what SparkleGirl had told him. "The closer we get to Herobrine the more hostile mobs we're going to be coming up against." Coming to two tunnels that branched in different directions, Emman chose the one that went downhill. If he was going to find lots of hostile mobs in the daytime, Emman presumed that going further underground was the best way to go. "Come on Wolfie2," Emman called out to SparkleGirl's dog. For once Emman found himself leading the way. Maybe that dogs got more sense than I do, Emman thought to himself, what player would willing run into Herobrine's lair by choice. Probably only an idiot.

Keeping the thoughts of SparkleGirl's death and ChuckBone's arrival in his mind, Emman fought back the fear that was building up in him and kept moving. He knew that if he stopped now he'd probably give up and go back. But if he could keep his mind busy on those two things he'd be able to keep his feet moving. Rounding a corner Emman eventually encountered his first hostile mob. Up ahead of him and coming his way was a zombie. Before the zombie had a chance to react to his presence, Emma plunged his sword into its chest and continued on running. "That wasn't so bad," Emman remarked to himself. Then before he had a chance to congratulate himself further he found his way ahead blocked. Three creepers that had been walking around aimlessly now turned in his direction and started to walk towards him. On seeing what was happening Wolfie2 now took the lead and growled at what he saw. Using the distraction that Wolfie2 had given him, Emman threw an Ender pearl over the creepers heads and instantly teleported behind them. Without taking a moment to think about what he was doing, Emman swung his sword wildly and cut two of the creepers across the back killing them instantly. The third creeper seeing what was happening quickly went into countdown mode and moved closer to Emman. "Oh no you don't!" Emman said to the creeper and plunged his sword into its belly.

Pulling his sword out Emman marvelled at what he'd done. "Wow, did you see that Wolfie2? Why it is that SparkleGirl's never around when I do something right. Darn she would have been impressed." Taking a moment to savour his victory, Emman turned around and froze in place. Looking at what was in front of him, Emman realized that no amount of Ender pearls would save him now.

# Chapter 12

"Game over," Emman said to himself. Looking at the huge group of hostile mobs that were now coming his way it certainly looked that way. "Get behind me Wolfie2," Emman said pulling SparkleGirl's dog behind him. "This is my fight Wolfie2, you just watch my back in case anything else comes from behind." Holding tight to the handle of his sword Emman held it out in front of him and then roared at the top of his voice, "HEROBRINE, HEROBRINE, I KNOW YOU'RE IN THERE SOMEWHERE, SHOW YOURSELF TO ME!"

While not the response he was looking for, Emman did get a response as the crowd of mobs started moving towards him at a faster rate. "That's not the answer I was looking for," Emman said to himself and started to slowly step backwards. "HEROBRINE, SHOW YOURSELF TO ME," Emman screamed again at the top of his lungs. As before he couldn't hear anything above the hissing and shuffling noises of the hostile mobs. "I'm sorry, I tried SparkleGirl," Emman said and got ready to fight.

With so many enemies coming towards him, Emman knew if he was to stand a chance of getting through this battle he would have to put the odds in his favour. Using the recent experience of the battle in the arena, Emman edged backwards until he could see the tunnel around him start to narrow. Smiling to himself, he could see that his plan was now working. Where once the hostile mobs had been six across at the front, the narrowness of the tunnel was forcing them down to only two. Taking the first two mobs on, Emman chopped at two zombies and killed them where they stood. After that the battle quickly became a blur of two more mobs replacing the one's in front that had been killed. "This isn't so bad," Emman called over his shoulder to Wolfie2. "That's as long as this sword holds up."

As Emman fought on, his mind began to wander to what was happening in the world outside the tunnel. Where was ChuckBone, had he landed on the beach yet? Had he brought his full army with him or was he only at half strength. And what about SparkleGirl, was she also making her way back to the island. After a while Emman could see he was starting to get nowhere. He wasn't any closer to finding Herobrine, and this fight was just wasting time. The clock was ticking. He needed to warn Herobrine as soon as possible if they were going to be able to stop ChuckBone. Looking at the endless amount of mobs coming at him it would only be a matter of time before he made a mistake. "Screw this," Emman said to himself. "This is your last chance Herobrine. If you don't answer me now it's your own fault."

Kicking an oncoming creeper back towards the group, Emman took this moment to scream out again. "HEROBRINE WHERE ARE YOU? SHOW YOURSELF, SPARKLEGIRL NEEDS YOUR HELP!" Emman scanned through the crowd of hostile mobs for any response, but as before there was nothing. "You know what, I'm really tried. I'm sorry SparkleGirl. I did my best but I guess that wasn't good enough," Emman said feeling dejected. Looking at the oncoming group still coming towards him Emman gave up hope and threw his sword to the ground. "I'm sorry Wolfie2, I'm sorry." Closing his eyes Emman braced himself for the quick flash of pain he'd receive before respawning back to his respawn point.

Waiting for death Emman counted in his head but nothing happened. "Huh," Emman said slowly opening his eyes and looking around him. He'd been expecting to see a hostile mob just about to finish him off but not this. Taking a moment to make sure he wasn't seeing things Emman opened and closed his eyes again. "Hey stranger," SparkleGirl said with a grin. "SparkleGirl how the, where were, I tried, oh God it's so good to see you again," Emman said running over to her and throwing his arms around her. "But how, you fell, how did you get here, I saw?" Emman said firing off one question after another. "Slow down there. Before we get to all of that there's someone I want you to meet," SparkleGirl said and held out her arm to the other player. "I think you know who he is."

Emman stood in shock with his mouth wide open. "Yep, that's Herobrine Emman. And by the way you can close your mouth now, you look like a goldfish," SparkleGirl said grinning. "What, yeah… Hi… Mr Herobrine," Emman said stuttering his words. "By the way, Herobrine here wants to kill you for what you did. Giving away his secret like that," SparkleGirl said with a straight face. "Oh God I'm sorry, I'm so sorry!" Emman pleaded and dropped to his knees. "Whatever you want I'll do it, to make up for my mistake. Please don't kill me!" "Get up you fool, I was only kidding,"

SparkleGirl said and started to roar with laughter. "What, that was a nasty trick you pulled there," Emman said getting up off the ground. "Think of it as payback," SparkleGirl chuckled. "Payback for what," Emman asked. "You know what for. For letting me fall into that cavern yesterday and almost getting blown up by a crowd of creepers. And then, here's the best part. You then bricked me up inside it," SparkleGirl added.

Emman's face began to flush with redness. "I, I, I thought you were dead. I really did. I looked down, and I thought you'd been blown up. I was so scared that I bricked it up. I'm so sorry SparkleGirl, really I am!" Emman pleaded again. "I know Emman. I should have let you know that I'd survived. I didn't want you getting hurt on my account and finding yourself in a situation... well like this," SparkleGirl said and pointed to all the hostile mobs that were now frozen in place. "Now enough about all of this," SparkleGirl remarked as she cleared her throat. "ChuckBone's just landed on the beach and we've got a battle to fight."

# Chapter 13

SparkleGirl, Emman and Herobrine lay down on a hillside overlooking the beach and watched all the activity below them. "There must be nearly two hundred players down there," Emman remarked to SparkleGirl as he watched ChuckBone pointing and giving orders. "What do you think he's saying?" "Who knows Emman, but you can bet our names have been mentioned a few times. That's for sure," SparkleGirl replied. Emman watched as Herobrine got up and moved away from beside her and walked back to talk to a group of hostile mobs.

"He doesn't talk much does he," Emman whispered to SparkleGirl. "Like all the time he's been with us, I haven't heard him speak once. Is he mad at me?" "Who, Herobrine," SparkleGirl remarked. "Nah, it's been that way since he changed. Whatever happened to him the day he took that potion, he's never spoken a word since. I don't think he can, tell the truth." "Aw, that's awful," Emman remarked looking back at Herobrine. "So what's the plan? Are we going to attack tonight when they're not expecting it?" Emman asked feeling more confident now that he was back with SparkleGirl. "Nope, we're just going to sit here and wait," SparkleGirl said with a grin. "What, look at him, he's setting up shelters on the beach and we're going to let him. Once they set up beds and stay the night, this island is going to be their respawning point, that's crazy. Why not kill them all now and then they'll end up back on the mainland again!" Emman protested. "And what good is that going to do Emman. Once they end up back on the mainland, they'll just keep coming back again and again. No, this fights going to start and end on this island. One way or another, either we don't make it or they don't. But this is where it's going to be decided," SparkleGirl stated and pointed her finger in the dirt.

SparkleGirl watched as some of the colour drained out of Emman's face. "You're scared aren't you," SparkleGirl asked Emman. "It's OK. I am too!" "That makes me even more scared. Now that you're scared," Emman trembled. "I know it looks bad Emman, I know. But we've got to fight. ChuckBone can't be allowed to win this fight. Once he gets his hands on Herobrine's power you know how he'll use it. He'll be unstoppable. At the moment Herobrine is trying to spawn as many hostile mobs as he can. That's another reason why we need an extra night. But even then we'll still be out numbered," SparkleGirl said and watched as Emman's shoulders started to drop.

"Hey, don't be glum. Look at it this way, if we win this fight, you'll become a legend! Imagine all the girls that'll want to be seen hanging out with you then!" SparkleGirl remarked with a smile. "Yeah. I never thought of it that way," Emman said breaking out into a wide grin. "Well hello ladies. What's my name? It's Emman. You might have heard of me around here," Emman said imaging himself surrounded with a group of girls. SparkleGirl gave Emman a playful punch in the arm to get his attention. "Hey knucklehead. Let's get moving, I think someone spotted us up here," SparkleGirl said and crawled away. Following SparkleGirl's lead, Emman crawled a short distance away before getting to his feet and joining her and Herobrine. "Come on Herobrine, we better move I think we've been spotted," SparkleGirl said and lead the way to a nearby cave.

*****

"I'll never get used to that," Emman said looking at all the hostile mobs walking around him. "What, you mean they're ignoring you. Yeah I know, it takes a while to get used to that. But as long as Herobrine's here they won't pay any attention to us. Just be aware that once he's not around, they'll turn on you in a second. So it's best to stay alert any time you're around them," SparkleGirl said. "You think they know where we're hiding," Emman asked. "Who ChuckBone, yeah probably, but he won't try anything tonight. I know he'll be itching to start this fight as soon as possible but he'll wait. To tell the truth I bet he's scared too. He's lost to Herobrine before and he won't want to lose a second time. That's what's going to make him more dangerous this time. He's going to try everything he can to win, and we need to be ready for that. Why don't you get some sleep now while you can Emman? It might be the last chance you get. I'll take first watch. Now off you go," SparkleGirl said and watched as Emman trudged grudgingly over to a bed he had built earlier and lay down next to Wolfie2.

SparkleGirl turned around when she heard Herobrine walk up behind her. "Will we be ready for him?" SparkleGirl asked. Herobrine held out his hand and did a maybe gesture with it. "It's going to be that close, is it,"

SparkleGirl asked. "But I know you well enough to know you've got something else up your sleeve. So what is it?" Herobrine just smiled back in response and tapped the side of his nose with his finger. "You don't trust me do you, you're probably right to keep it to yourself? You can see what happened when your last secret got out," SparkleGirl said and pointed to the situation they were now in. "But I hope it works. And like I said earlier I'm sorry about all of this. I wonder if they'll ever be a time when I won't find myself standing beside you other than in battle." Herobrine smiled again, put his hand on her shoulder and then returned to work with the hostile mobs.

"I hope you know what you're doing Herobrine," SparkleGirl whispered as she watched him at work. "Because I wouldn't bet on us right now."

# Chapter 14

SparkleGirl and Emman returned to the spot they had been at the previous day and again watched the activity in the camp below. "Well todays the day," Emman remarked. "I wonder what Chucky's got planned for us." "That's a good one, Chucky. He doesn't seem as mean when you call him that," SparkleGirl said. "Well are you ready? You know what to do, don't you Emman?" "Come on, I may be a bit dim at times, but we've been over this again and again, I know what I'm doing." "OK off you go and I'll watch your back," SparkleGirl said and gave Emman a nudge. "And give Chucky my love if you see him."

SparkleGirl watched as Emman made his way down to ChuckBone's camp as quietly as he could before pausing to give her a thumbs up signal. Reaching into her inventory SparkleGirl took out a handful of arrows and placed them on the ground beside her. It didn't take long before Emman was discovered, but that didn't happen until he'd taken out two of ChuckBone's players with two killing shots. Now he was running for his life towards SparkleGirl with almost twenty players in tow.

Ignoring Emman's plea's to shoot straight away, SparkleGirl took her time before unleashing her first arrow. Instantly a player who almost had Emman, fell to the ground dead with an arrow in the chest. From then on she picked off five more players before they stopped in their tracks and started to return fire. Ducking her head down to avoid the flying arrows, SparkleGirl grabbed Emman's arm and pulled him to safety behind a rock.

"Well... you... took... your... time... they... almost... had... me," Emman gasped as he tried to catch his breath and speak at the same time. "You're just not fit Emman. Out of breath after a short run like that. I thought I was going to have to go down there and carry you on my shoulders" SparkleGirl replied and started to chuckle. "Are we moving or what," Emman asked as another arrow ricocheted off the rock they were behind. "I was waiting on you," SparkleGirl said and pulled Emman to his feet and dragged him after her.

Running towards a nearby cave SparkleGirl could tell without looking that the group of angry players had grown. It didn't surprise her, a group of angry players respawning in camp was bound to get everyone's attention. Once inside the cave SparkleGirl and Emman could hear the voices behind them growing more distant. "Looks like they're waiting for reinforcement," Emman gulped. "Or waiting for ChuckBone's orders," SparkleGirl added "But whatever happens, we can't let them lose us. Best get your sword out." Packing her bow away and taking out her sword SparkleGirl and Emman waited until they heard the first heavy footfalls of their pursuers before running again. "COME AND CATCH US IF YOU CAN!" SparkleGirl roared back over her shoulder. "Did you have to do that? Don't you think they're angry enough already," Emman groaned. "Just stirring the pot a little," SparkleGirl replied with a smile "Now come on."

Where once the mouth of the cave had a wide opening it soon began to narrow into tunnels that were only the width of one player. "Nearly there," SparkleGirl said as they rounded a sharp corner. "Time to slow down and let them catch us." "This is the bit I don't like," Emman replied slowing down. Once around the last corner Emman and SparkleGirl found themselves in a large cavern that could easily hold up to fifty players in it. Walking to the back wall SparkleGirl and Emman turned to face the group of players that had started to pour into the cavern. "Oh, no, we're trapped," SparkleGirl called out when she saw the first player come in. "Please don't kill us, we're sorry." SparkleGirl watched as the face of the player changed from confusion to a smirk. "HEY THEY'RE TRAPPED, ITS A DEAD END!" the player shouted back to the players coming behind him. "I hope you know what you're doing SparkleGirl," Emman whispered to SparkleGirl as the cavern quickly filled up with ChuckBone's players.

"She's trapped ChuckBone," a voice called out at the back of the group. Watching the group part, SparkleGirl saw ChuckBone striding confidently to the front of the group. "Trapped like a rat," ChuckBone cheered. "You pushed your luck this time SparkleGirl. Now where's Herobrine? Maybe I'll let you go if you tell me. Now where is he?" "I'm sorry SparkleGirl I can't do this anymore," Emman groaned "If you want Herobrine I can tell you where he is." "Good man, now where is he?" ChuckBone replied with a smirk. "HE'S RIGHT HERE!" Emman roared out. Before ChuckBone or anyone in his group had a chance to react, Herobrine suddenly teleported into the cavern with four creepers. Then grabbing SparkleGirl and

Emman's hand's the three players vanished out of sight.

Watching the four creepers walk to the far wall and then flash on and off. ChuckBone screamed out as loud as he could, "IT'S A TRAP, IT'S A TRAP!" At once panic broke out in ChuckBone's group as players fought with each other to get back into the narrow opening of the tunnel. Looking back to the creepers ChuckBone could see they'd never all escape. He then watched as the creepers exploded through the cavern wall releasing a huge wave of molten lava that swept away everything in front of it.

# Chapter 15

"What I wouldn't have given to see the look on Chucky's face when that wall came down," Emman said to SparkleGirl with a chuckle. "You know that it's not over Emman. We may have won this battle but not the war. What we did was just slow ChuckBone down for a while and give us some time. But he's going to come back hard at us for that. We just showed him up in front of his players and he won't be too happy about that." "Yeah I suppose so, I hadn't thought of it like that. So what's next?" Emman asked eagerly. "Nothing we just sit and wait," SparkleGirl replied. "While it's great to have all those hostile mobs at our control, we won't be able to do anything until the sun goes down. Unfortunately ChuckBone knows that as well and he'll be waiting for us."

Emman got up from where he was sitting and paced up and down. "What's wrong, can't wait to get started?" SparkleGirl asked as she watched him. "Nah, it's just being down here. I think this is the longest time I've spent underground and it's starting to get to me. I'm a bit stir crazy at the moment," Emman said and continued pacing. "I'll tell you what, why don't you take Wolfie2 top side with you. It'll give him a chance to stretch his legs. But don't go wandering off. ChuckBone's still out there so watch your back. The first sign of trouble and you get back here, you hear me? And don't go far we'll be moving out soon," SparkleGirl ordered. "Yes ma'am!" Emman replied with a grin and went to fetch Wolfie2.

*****

Emman stood at the mouth of the cave and took in a deep breath of fresh air. It felt good to be above ground and away from the confined space and hostile mobs. Emman had never noticed before how much hostile mobs stank until now. Whether it was the rotting flesh of the zombies or something worse, there always seemed to be a smell hanging around in the tunnels. Emman wondered how Herobrine put up with it, maybe like his speech he'd lost his sense of smell too. Whatever it was, it still made Emman's skin crawl hanging around them.

Emman watched Wolfie2 as he stretched the kinks out of his back and then took off running around to burn up some surplus energy. "Suffering from cabin fever too boy? I know how you feel. I thought I was the only one starting to crack up down there?" Emman remarked. Wolfie2 let out a bark in response and in a giddy fit ran over and back in front of Emman. "You wanna play? Alright then, but you heard SparkleGirl, not too far away. And any sign of trouble and we come straight back here, you hear me?" Wolfie2 didn't wait for a response and took off running through the tree's leaving Emman far behind him. "Darn you dog wait for me," Emman cried out in frustration.

While Emman had been angry at the dog for a while, it wasn't long before he too was enjoying the freedom of running around over ground. "Thanks Wolfie2 I needed that," Emman said as he caught up with the dog. "Come on we better get a move on. The sun's starting to go down and it won't be long before this battle kicks off. Let's go." Reaching down to grab onto Wolfie2's collar, SparkleGirl's dog suddenly took off again and vanished over a hill. "Aw come on, this isn't funny anymore!" Emman cried out and ran to catch up with Wolfie2.

Taking a moment to admire the view from the next hilltop, Emman stopped to catch his breath and look around him. If they didn't have the problem with ChuckBone to take care of Emman was starting to enjoy life on the island. Looking at the sun going down on the horizon Emman pushed that thought away. Now he had to find SparkleGirl's dog. "Now where is that dog?" Emman asked looking off in all directions. He knew he'd better find him soon or SparkleGirl would kill him. Walking down the hill in the direction he thought Wolfie2 might have gone Emman found himself on the beach. That was it, Wolfie2 was only getting one more minute of search time and then he was leaving him behind. It was too dangerous being out here.

Resigned to the fact that Wolfie2 didn't want to be found, Emman turned around and started to walk back the way he'd came. Grumbling to himself and coming up with a story to tell SparkleGirl, he never noticed the cave until he was standing in front of it. Wondering how he hadn't seen it earlier, he walked over to check it out. In the last rays of daylight Emman could make out some shapes inside. Walking closer he recognised the shapes, it was boats and lots of them. Emman froze in place when he realized what he was looking at. "Oh God, we're in trouble," Emman gulped to himself. "ChuckBone's got more players here than we thought. We're not prepared for a fight like this. Sod it dog you can stay here!" His mind filled with panic Emman didn't hear the two players come up from behind him until it was too late.

# Chapter 16

"Are you ready?" SparkleGirl whispered over to Herobrine. Herobrine nodded his head and waved his arm forward. From their position SparkleGirl and Herobrine watched as the first hostile mobs headed into ChuckBone's camp. As SparkleGirl watched what was happening below her she wondered where Emman was. At the start she'd been worried about his absence but now she was glad that he wasn't here. Although he was a good friend, this battle wasn't his to fight, and she didn't want to see him get hurt because of her. This was between them and ChuckBone and no one else. Inside SparkleGirl felt sorry for the players that were about to be killed tonight. But that was something she couldn't do anything about. Unfortunately they had tied their flag to ChuckBone's mast, and they were going to pay for it.

It didn't take long before the players in the camp below noticed what was happening to them and sprang into action. Once Herobrine could see that the first wave of mobs were starting to be cut down he sent in the next group. SparkleGirl marvelled as a group of skeletons ran down the hill as fast as they could go and then once in range, started to fire off their arrows. Now the balance of the fight was starting to go in Herobrine's favour. Keen to get into the fight SparkleGirl pulled a handful of arrows out of her inventory and then checked her bow string. She and Herobrine would be going in the third wave.

As SparkleGirl watched the fight unfold in the camp below, she wondered where ChuckBone was. Surely he'd be leading the charge by now and fighting up front, but there was no sign of him. But then thinking it over SparkleGirl realized that this was typical ChuckBone. He'd send all his players to their deaths and sit back to watch. Then when he was sure of a win he'd step forward and take the glory. Just thinking about him made SparkleGirl's blood boil and she couldn't wait to find him. She knew by right it should be Herobrine that sorted him out, but if she came across him first she might do it herself. Herobrine looked over at SparkleGirl and nodded his head, it was time.

Loading her first arrow into her bow SparkleGirl and Herobrine joined a large group of creepers and spiders and started their approach. With her adrenaline now pumping in her body SparkleGirl could feel the familiar sensation of time starting to slow down. Pulling her bow string back she watched as her arrow slowly left her bow and then in what seemed like an age hit her first target. SparkleGirl watched as the player fell onto his back with an arrow in his chest. Loading her bow again she picked her second target, a player that was fighting off a skeleton, and sent an arrow in his direction. Now almost on the edge of camp SparkleGirl looked for her third target and took out a player that was running towards her with his sword drawn.

Packing away her bow and taking out her sword SparkleGirl took a second to pause and look around her. Where was everyone she wondered? Yesterday they had presumed that this fight would have gone on for most of the night but now it looked like it was almost over. SparkleGirl didn't like it, this was too easy. Looking over to see how Herobrine was getting on, she could see he too was without an enemy to fight.

Now confused SparkleGirl ran different scenarios through her mind. Could ChuckBone have given up and run away, she didn't think so, Herobrine's power meant too much to him. Maybe his players had deserted him after the lava attack. Or maybe he'd taken some of his players out on patrol and not come back yet. Whatever was happening her instincts were telling her to get the hell out of there. Running to Herobrine to tell him how she felt, they both turned when they saw a lone player running out of camp. "Quick after him, but don't kill him. We need to know what's going on," SparkleGirl ordered and gave chase.

While she'd been expecting a chase before catching the player, she was surprised when he gave up easily. Turning around with his sword drawn SparkleGirl knocked it easily out of his hand. "OK where's ChuckBone?" SparkleGirl commanded and advanced towards the player with her sword pointed at his chest. "He's not here," the player replied with a grin. "I can see that for myself, so where is he?" SparkleGirl barked and stepped even closer. Watching the player SparkleGirl could see that he was paying more attention to Herobrine than her. "Ever met Herobrine before? I doubt it, he'd probably have killed you if you did. Well have a good look at him because if you don't tell me where ChuckBone is I'm walking away from here and you two can chat. This is your last chance, where's ChuckBone?" "You can't scare me, you or him. It should be you that's scared of me," the player replied with a sneer. SparkleGirl laughed when she heard this. "Oh yeah, and how is it we should be scared of you?" "Because of this!" the player said and stepped backwards onto a pressure plate. "Say goodbye to your hostile mobs."

Confused SparkleGirl and Herobrine turned their attention away from the player and back to the campsite. Without warning the first TNT charge erupted followed by a chain reaction of explosions that broke out all over the campsite. Knocked to the ground by the force of the blast, SparkleGirl watched as the player ran off and then shook her head to clear it. Getting up she and Herobrine stood dumbfounded at the crater and burning ruin that now stood before them. All their hard work and hostile mobs were gone, wiped out in an instant.

"You're not the only one that can set up a good trap SparkleGirl. Now give up, you're surrounded." Without turning around, SparkleGirl knew ChuckBone had a huge grin on his face.

# Chapter 17

"Oh I do love a good fireworks display, don't you?" ChuckBone asked with a grin. "Why the long face SparkleGirl, if I didn't know better I'd think you weren't pleased to see me. And you Herobrine, did it hurt seeing all those hostile mobs die like that?" "You scum," SparkleGirl spat and stepped forward with her sword raised. "Really, look around you SparkleGirl do you honestly think you'd get to use that thing on me. You'd be killed before you took another step. Admit it you've been beaten. I know you don't like to lose but honestly face the facts SparkleGirl, you're surrounded and your army of hostile mobs is gone, just give up." "Never! As long as there's a breath in my body I'll never let you win. And what about you lot?" SparkleGirl said and turned her attention to the players standing beside ChuckBone, "Do you honestly think you can trust him. He's just using you all and you can't even see it. Once he's got what he wants he won't need you anymore. Think about it."

SparkleGirl looked at all the blank faces in the glow of the torches and sighed when no one responded to her. "See I told you, you've been beaten now surrender!" ChuckBone commanded. Out of the corner of her eye SparkleGirl watched as Herobrine moved his hand closer towards hers. "I DARE YOU TO TRY IT HEROBRINE!" ChuckBone roared. "But I don't think SparkleGirl will want to go with you this time. Not when she sees who I have here." With that ChuckBone stepped aside and a player from the back of the group walked forward with Wolfie2 on a lead. "NO, DON'T YOU DARE LAY A FINGER ON HIM!" SparkleGirl screamed. "Maybe I will, maybe I won't?" ChuckBone said and held onto Wolfie2's lead. "But if you teleport out of here with him I'm killing your dog. You know I'll do it, don't you Herobrine. Remember how I killed your dog before."

SparkleGirl watched as Herobrine took his arm back and kept it by his side. "That's better," ChuckBone said with a grin. "Oh by the way I never got a chance to introduce my army to you. A nice group as you can see, three hundred players at last count. Amazing isn't it, how many people hate you Herobrine. Oh I know there may be some in this group who aren't my biggest fans but they still hate you more Herobrine." "A bunch of idiots if you ask me," SparkleGirl replied looking at all the faces in the group. "Yes Herobrine may have caused some trouble in the past but you were to blame for it ChuckBone, just as much as he was. It was because of you that he took that potion that changed him. He may have become a monster, but you were one a long time before he was." "Listen to her you're a fine one to point the finger SparkleGirl," ChuckBone stated. "How many players have you killed since we first met, one hundred, two hundred? You've probably lost count. Take a look in the mirror SparkleGirl before you go calling anyone a monster." At that SparkleGirl fell quiet. Although she didn't want to admit it, ChuckBone had a point. Since she'd left his group she'd made a lot of enemies and killed a lot of players on the way. Some deserved it, some didn't, but he was right she had become a monster like him.

"Now enough of all this name calling, you know what we're here for Herobrine," ChuckBone said and pulled out his sword. "Did you know I had this specially made just for you? Like you it's a bit special, any wound you receive off this sword will be a mortal wound and one you'll never recover from. I promise this won't hurt a bit, just a quick chop and it'll all be over." SparkleGirl looked from Herobrine to ChuckBone and wondered if this was how it was going to end. Surely it couldn't be as easy as ChuckBone simply walking up to Herobrine and chopping off his head. She couldn't allow that to happen. "RUN HEROBRINE, RUN!" SparkleGirl screamed. "DON'T WORRY ABOUT ME, SAVE YOURSELF!"

SparkleGirl stood in shock and watched as Herobrine stood his ground and held up his hand to silence her. It was going to happen, he was going to give up his life for her, and there was nothing she could do about it. "Please Herobrine, you can't let him win don't do this, not for me!" SparkleGirl sobbed and wiped away the tears that were now falling down her cheeks. Even though she wanted to close her eyes to what was about to happen SparkleGirl watched as ChuckBone walked over to Herobrine and then raised his sword for a killing blow. "Goodbye Herobrine," ChuckBone said with a grin.

Without warning an arrow came from behind SparkleGirl and pierced ChuckBone in his shoulder making him drop his sword. "Arrrgghh!" ChuckBone screamed and looked at the shaft of the arrow that was now sticking out of his body. Before anyone had a chance to react to what had happened, Herobrine grabbed the fallen sword and held it to ChuckBone's throat. "Well I didn't see that coming, SparkleGirl said with a grin. "I don't think I have to tell you all, what will happen if any of you move a muscle. Isn't that right ChuckBone." SparkleGirl watched as ChuckBone nodded his head in agreement and held up his hands to his players. "Glad we got that sorted. Now I think I'll be taking my dog back, thank you," SparkleGirl said and watched as the player released his grip on Wolfie2. Picking up Wolfie2 in her arms SparkleGirl walked to Herobrine and spoke to ChuckBone. "You know I only have to say the word and he'll cut your head off, don't you. Then like you said, it'll be game over. We're leaving now but I promise if you keep this up it's not going to end well for you. Come on Herobrine."

Lifting his leg Herobrine pushed ChuckBone in the back with his foot and sent him flying to the ground in front of his players. Then before anyone had a chance to move he grabbed SparkleGirl's hand and they teleported away.

# Chapter 18

"That was a hell of a shot back there," SparkleGirl exclaimed to Emman. "It would have been if it had hit its target," Emman added his face starting to blush. "I was aiming for his head, not his shoulder." "Thank God you didn't hit it. If you'd killed him back there we wouldn't have been able to use him to get away. I don't think it would have worked as well using a dead body as a hostage," SparkleGirl said and started to giggle. "So what happened before Herobrine came back to get you?" SparkleGirl asked. "Well first there was a lot of shouting. Some of ChuckBone's army didn't take it well when he went to pieces like that. Someone called him a coward and then it all kicked off. The last thing I saw was some of ChuckBone's close friends trying to protect him with their swords drawn. It didn't look good for ChuckBone back there. But the thing I don't understand is why didn't you kill him. You had your chance and you let him go. If it was me, I'd probably have done it SparkleGirl?" Emman said looking confused.

"Believe me the thought had crossed my mind but after what he'd said it got me thinking. Was I really turning into a monster, was I really getting as bad as he was. Herobrine hadn't a choice the way he ended up, but me I did. Having Herobrine take off ChuckBone's head wouldn't have made a difference at all. In some ways it might have made things a lot worse for us. ChuckBone would suddenly become a martyr to that lot out there. A hero that they'd have to get revenge for. But now they've all seen him for the coward that he is. They could see the fear in his eyes and in that instant he'd lost them. That's why I let him go," SparkleGirl said. "But wait you didn't tell me how you came to be up there, taking that shot?"

"That's a long story. But to be quick, after I lost Wolfie2 I found lots of boats on the beach and knew we were in trouble. Then I ran into two of ChuckBone's players, who luckily for me, were worse with a sword than I was. Maybe that's why they were guarding the boats. Well anyway after I finished them off I raced back here and you were gone. Then I heard the explosion and knew you were in trouble. After that I don't know what came over me but I knew you'd need my help. Then by the time I got down there, ChuckBone was about to take Herobrine's head and well you know the rest," Emman said and drew a deep breath. "If that's the short version, I'd have hate to have heard the long version," SparkleGirl said and started to laugh.

Hearing a noise behind her SparkleGirl turned to see Herobrine coming towards her. "Well how does it look?" SparkleGirl asked. Herobrine bent down to pick up a stick and then drew in the dirt at his feet. "You say half of them have given up and are returning to their boats," SparkleGirl said looking first at the picture on the ground and then to Herobrine. "That's still a lot of players to fight against Herobrine and we don't have any hostile mobs to call on. There's no way we could fight thirty or forty players each and win. So what do we do? I don't know about you but I think it's time we got off this island Herobrine. Let's just run and get far away from here." Herobrine turned back to his drawing on the ground and dug furiously at it again and again with his stick. "I know, I know, you're right. We'll never get free if we don't take a stand here. I know they'll keep coming after us, but come on Herobrine we'll die here if we stay!" SparkleGirl pleaded to Herobrine.

Suddenly Herobrine broke into a grin and SparkleGirl could see his body language change. "You've got something, an idea, well what is it?" SparkleGirl asked with excitement and watched as Herobrine disappeared. "God I hate it when he does that!" SparkleGirl moaned turning her attention back to Emman. "You're a fine one to complain you're always doing that to me. Now I know where you get it from," Emman smirked and ducked as SparkleGirl swung a playful punch at him.

"So what do you think happened out there," Emman asked. "What do you mean, to ChuckBone's group," SparkleGirl asked. "Who knows but I guess some of the players got sense and realized what they were getting into. Maybe other ones realized ChuckBone wasn't the big hero he was making himself out to be. Then there were probably others who had just come along for the ride, you know to say they'd been there when Herobrine was killed. You know those type of players. But the last group, the ones that are staying, they're the real ones we need to worry about. They're here to get revenge on Herobrine and maybe even me. They're the ones we need to worry about."

Emman gave an audible gulping noise when he heard the last thing

SparkleGirl had said. "But come on we've been in tough scrapes before Emman. We'll get through this too. Have some fate in the big guy." Right on cue Herobrine reappeared holding three small potion flasks in his hands and a huge grin on his face. "Maybe it's just me but I think he's happy about something," SparkleGirl said to Emman. "When he grins like that, is it a good sign or a bad sign, I can never tell," Emman asked sounding worried. "From experience it usually means it's good for us and bad for someone else. Maybe things aren't going to be as bad as you'd feared Emman." Without another word Herobrine grabbed on to SparkleGirl and Emman and teleported them far from their underground hideout.

# Chapter 19

"Look there they go!" Emman said excitedly as he watched boats heading off towards the horizon. "I never thought we'd be alive to see that sight SparkleGirl." "Yeah I know, but it's not over yet Emman. There's still plenty of players who'd love to get their hands on us," SparkleGirl said pointing down towards the players that were scouring the island below them. "Do you think they'll fall for the same trick twice? I mean could they be that dumb," Emman asked. "Who knows let's see what happens," SparkleGirl said. "Right let's go."

SparkleGirl and Emman raced down to some trees that were close to their targets and hid. With a nod of her head to Emman, SparkleGirl stood away from her hiding place, took aim with her bow and killed a player where he stood. Confused the players ran for cover but not until Emman had taken another player out with an arrow in his back. "Over there in the trees, it's them, quick tell the others!" a player called out. SparkleGirl hid back behind her tree just before an arrow went whistling by where her head had been. With another nod of her head SparkleGirl watched as Emman retreated and raced to another tree further back. Reloading her bow, SparkleGirl jumped out again from behind her tree and took out a player that was aiming at Emman. Now back in hiding she watched as Emman made it to his new position before a group of arrows hit the ground where he'd been standing.

Peeking her head out from behind her tree, SparkleGirl could see that the small group that they had attacked was growing rapidly. To the left and right players were coming running in support and were now racing up the hill towards her. "This is going to be close," SparkleGirl remarked to herself. Placing some TNT on the ground she waited until Emman gave the signal and then punched it. Seeing the first flash of the TNT block she knew she wouldn't have much time and ran away as fast as she could.

Diving for cover beside Emman, SparkleGirl lay on the ground and listened to the confusion that her TNT had made. "I think that really made them mad," Emman remarked, "You took out three players with that blast." Getting up SparkleGirl looked at their pursuers and remarked at how quickly the group was still growing. "I think someone needs to talk to

Herobrine about his math, that's a lot more players than we were expecting. Quick run for it and join Herobrine in the cave!" Setting down two more TNT charges SparkleGirl waited until Emman was clear before punching them and running after him. SparkleGirl watched in relief as Emman reached the safety of the cave before an intense pain tore through her body. Falling to the ground she watched as the expression on Emman's faced changed to complete horror as he watched what was happening in front of him. Hitting the ground she knew she was in trouble, when a second arrow tore into her body. Reeling in pain SparkleGirl screamed out to Emman to get Herobrine before closing her eyes to fight the pain in her body.

"Well, well, well, good to see you again SparkleGirl," a voice spoke before SparkleGirl felt a hard kick in her side. "Turn her over and let me look at her." As SparkleGirl was turned around she came face to face with someone she hadn't seen in a while, MaxDan. "Oh, surprised to see me. You didn't think I'd just walk away after what you did to me, did you? I told you I'd get my revenge and now here we are. ChuckBone paid for what he did to me too. Making himself out to be the big hero, but then we all saw what he was like, a coward. He looked to be in a lot of pain before he died. In fact he looked a lot like you do right now.

Does it hurt SparkleGirl?" MaxDan asked in false pity as he pushed down on an arrow shaft that was sticking out of her leg. "I hope it does, but it'll soon be over. You see those arrow tips were coated in the same material as that sword we had planned to use on Herobrine. In fact even as we speak that arrow head is dissolving and slowly poisoning every part of your body. I'd give you maybe twenty minutes. ChuckBone didn't last much longer. I'd love to stay and watch but you know how it is. So many people to kill, I don't expect it will be long before Herobrine and that coward Emman will be joining you. So farewell SparkleGirl, it was fun killing you," MaxDan sneered and ran off to join the rest of the players that were chasing after Emman.

*****

Running through the tunnel Emman's mind was filled with panic and dread. Their plan the one that they were sure was going to work, was now in tatters. SparkleGirl was wounded and God only knew what they were doing to her, was she even alive anymore. Running as fast as he could,

Emman knew he needed to get to Herobrine as soon as possible if SparkleGirl was to face any chance of staying alive. Once he rounded the last bend Emman found Herobrine waiting for him in a large cavern. "Hero… brine… Hero… brine… its Sparkle… Girl she's been shot, she's wounded," Emman stammered trying to get his breath back. "She was… coming after me… but she got shot… she's out there… wounded… help!"

Although Herobrine had a face that was hard to read Emman could see it change. Where once his eyes burned bright, they now took on a white hot intensity that scared Emman. Herobrine beckoned Emman to come stand behind him when the first players came in. Pulling out the sword he had taken off ChuckBone, Herobrine teleported into the middle of the group and unleashed hell on them. Emman stood and watched as Herobrine used the anger that was now in him to take on more players than Emman thought possible. Player after player fell to the ground, some with heads missing, others with body parts chopped off and others wandering around with open stab wounds. But while he had the advantage for a while, the sheer number of players that were pressing down on him in the tunnel started to change the odds in their favour. Then Emman watched in disbelief as Herobrine was swallowed up by the group and the battle moved back up the tunnel and out of sight.

# Chapter 20

Emman pulled out his sword and wondered what he should do next. Should he try to dig his way out of the cavern to escape or should he throw himself into the fight and hope he could make a difference. Not knowing what to do next Emman froze in place when he heard a voice cry out, "ARRRGHHH ZOMBIES!"

"Zombies," Emman remarked to himself "How, we don't have any more hostile mobs left on the island." Wondering how someone could have made that mistake Emman then heard other players screaming the same thing as well. "THEY'RE EVERYWHERE, GET BACK, GET BACK!" one player screamed. "WE CAN'T THEY'RE BEHIND US AS WELL!" another player roared back in response. Running up the tunnel to where the fight was, Emman stopped and stared at what was in front of him. It was true, there were zombies everywhere. Wondering what to do next, Emman then caught sight of Herobrine. There was no mistaking it he was still alive. In the middle of the fight two eyes burned brightly turning left and right along with a sword that was still chopping its way through the players. But where once he had been on his own, there were zombies now by his side biting and tearing their way through the players. Emman stood and watched in awe as Herobrine used the potions he had shown earlier and was splashing it onto players transforming them into zombies. These new zombies now turned ferociously on their fellow players and attacked them killing them where they stood.

Emman watched as the sea of green zombies grew in size and before long overcame all of ChuckBone's army and swallowed them up. Now that they'd won Herobrine put away his sword and walked back to Emman. On seeing Herobrine come toward him Emman held his head in shame and cried out, "I'm sorry, I chickened out. I didn't know what to do, and I just froze. There were some many, and I was so scared… I'm sorry!" Putting his hand on Emman's shoulder Herobrine gave it a squeeze as if to say that he understood and it was OK. Then holding Emman's hand Herobrine teleported them out of the tunnel.

On getting his bearings back after their teleportation, Emman ran to the spot where he had last seen SparkleGirl. "HEROBRINE OVER HERE, SHE'S HURT BAD I THINK SHE'S DEAD!" Emman roared back over his shoulder. Putting his hand on SparkleGirl's face, Emman tapped it gently and looked for any type of response. With nothing showing Emman broke down in tears and slumped his head down on top of her chest. "I'm sorry SparkleGirl, you were always there for me and when you needed me the most I ran like a coward!" Sobbing uncontrollably Emman felt Herobrine's strong hand on his shoulder and moved back off SparkleGirl's body. "It's no use Herobrine she's gone!" Emman spluttered looking at SparkleGirl's lifeless body.

Moving Emman off a little distance, Herobrine looked over SparkleGirl's body and examined her wounds. Taking a look and then sniffing them, Herobrine then pulled out ChuckBone's sword and smelt it as well. Emman watched in confusion at what was going on and thought Herobrine had also lost his mind with grief. "She's gone Herobrine, she's gone!" Emman repeated hoping this would help him see sense. Herobrine held up his hand as if to say be quiet and then he lowered his head to her chest. "What is it Herobrine, do you hear something?" Emman asked and jumped to his feet. Emman watched as Herobrine again held up his hand and listened intently to SparkleGirl's chest. "Well, what is it, what is it, is she still alive," Emman asked getting more animated and excited. Herobrine rose to his feet and nodded his head in response.

"YES!" Emman screamed in excitement. "Well what are we waiting for, you must have a health potion on you, give it to her quickly." Herobrine shook his head in the negative. Emman watched as Herobrine pointed at ChuckBone's sword and then to the wounds on SparkleGirl's body. "What are you saying they're the same? Oh God no. You heard him Herobrine, they're mortal wounds she's never going to recover from that." Emman felt his brief glimpse of hope being smashed by a sledgehammer of defeat into nothing. "So that's that then. She's going to die here and there's nothing you and I can do for her. There must be, there must be. You must have some type of magic spell or something that can stop that stuff? Think Herobrine think!"

Emman watched as Herobrine reached into his inventory and pulled out a small potion bottle. "So what's that Herobrine?" Emman asked. "One of those cure all potions?" Emman watched as Herobrine pointed first to himself and then to the potion. "You've got to be kidding me, right. I said save her not kill her. There's got to be something else we can do. Think, Herobrine, think!" Herobrine again shook his head in the negative and using his finger started to write in the dirt. "If I don't do this now, she'll die and we'll never get her back. It's our only hope!"

Emman read and reread the words over and over again and then finally admitted defeat. "OK so be it, but if we do this we can change her back, right?" Herobrine held up his hand horizontally and gave it a maybe shake. "There has to be, I won't stop searching all of Minecraft until I can find a way to change her back. You hear me!" Emman demanded. Herobrine nodded his head and placed the potion bottle to SparkleGirl's lips. Within seconds SparkleGirl's body shook uncontrollably and then stopped and lay still. When Emman saw SparkleGirl's eyes open he stepped back in fear and wondered if she'd ever forgive them for what they had done to her. Gone were the blue eyes he had known and now they were replaced by two white orbs of light like Herobrine.

She'd become a monster.

The End...

## Bonus Chapter from Emman - Hunt For a Monster

"I told you, I don't know anything," the player stammered looking down at the sword that was being held to his throat. "Really, I don't know anything, I swear." Herobrine lowered his sword and grabbed the player by the front of clothes, pulling him close to his face. "Honestly, I don't know anything," the player pleaded squirming against Herobrine's grip. Judging by the way the player was reacting, Herobrine knew he was wasting his time here. With a sigh of frustration, Herobrine pushed the player backwards and watched as he lost balance and fell on his behind. This was the third player he'd questioned today and still nothing. Was he ever going to find a cure for SparkleGirl? Angry about his lack of success, Herobrine snarled one last time at his victim before teleporting away to find his next informant.

*****

Standing across the road from "The Tavern" Herobrine pulled his hood up over his head and put on a pair of dark glasses. He knew it wasn't much of a disguise but getting his hands on the next player wouldn't be as easy as the last one. Pressing the glasses as close to his face as possible to hide his glowing eyes, Herobrine waited until a group of players entered the building and merged in with them. It was safer this way. Not that he feared getting hurt by anyone, but just that he wanted to get in without drawing attention to himself. People who hung out at The Tavern weren't big into strangers dropping by unannounced and Herobrine was in no mood on taking on everyone in a fight.

Once inside, Herobrine broke away from the group and made his way over to one of the tables in a darkened corner. Moving his chair so he had a clear view of both the entrance and exit, Herobrine sat down. Picking up a menu he tried to make himself look like any of the other regulars inside. Half looking at the menu and scanning the room at the same time, Herobrine could see his informant hadn't been in yet. "So what'll it be stranger?" a voice called out from beside him. Herobrine turned and noticed a waitress cleaning a table beside him. "I'd recommend the fish, we've got a great cook here who can do wonders with it." Not wanting to draw any attention to himself Herobrine gave her a thumbs up and a nod of his head. "OK, fish it is then, I'll be back with some water for your table."

Although he'd hadn't given much thought to his hunger as he'd been so busy chasing down a cure for SparkleGirl. The thought of some cooked fish was starting to make his mouth water. Watching his waitress walk away after dropping off his water, Herobrine took a long drink and started to feel him begin to relax. Maybe his luck would get better after he had a hot meal in him. That thought quickly passed when his name come up in conversation at a nearby table.

"He's dead and I know that for a fact. Whatever you might have thought of ChuckBone, he did it. He killed Herobrine once and for all." "You're a liar you know that. You're really telling us Herobrine's dead." Hearing his name mentioned a second time, Herobrine stopped what he was doing and started to listen in on the conversation that was happening two tables away from him. "Really, cross my heart, ChuckBone ran him underground like a rat and cornered him. They said he was begging for his life before ChuckBone cut his head off. God, I wish I'd been there to see that," the player remarked to himself. "How do you know all this?" another player called out. "You weren't there, and I haven't seen or heard anything about ChuckBone since he left for that island. He's still missing as far as I know." "It's true, I'm telling you Herobrine's dead and he ain't coming back. ChuckBone used some kind of sword on him that took him out of the game forever."

Hearing that last comment Herobrine knew he didn't need his informant anymore. Whoever this player was and whatever he knew, this was the guy he needed to be talking to. The guy might have had his facts mixed up, but he knew about the sword and no one else seemed to. Then as if reading his mind another player from the group piped up and asked the question Herobrine wanted to know as well.

"So how do you know all about this sword, you weren't even there," a player asked hoping to ruin the first player's tale. "OK, he told me to keep it quiet, so keep this to yourselves. OK. My brother TomKong was at the battle, but he was one of the ones who fled the place before the final battle took place. Yeah, I know he's a coward but what can you do. Anyway, when he was there he was talking to a guy, one of ChuckBone's head guys who knew all about the sword and gave him a glimpse of it. He said it looked amazing, it was like nothing he'd ever saw before. Well anyway, the guy told him that this was the sword that was going to kill Herobrine once and for all. Something about giving him a mortal wound or something or other. But like I said, keep this to yourselves. I shouldn't even be saying this to you. If TomKong found out he'd kill me," the player said, loving his moment in the spotlight.

"So where did it come from, this sword that looked like no other sword?" another player called out in a mocking tone. "This is just another of your tall tales. And why is it we're listening to this story from you and not from your brother if he was there. Where is he then?" "He's been keeping his head down since he came back. Says he's ashamed of himself for chickening out like that and running away. That's all I know, he didn't tell me everything, but I bet he knows where the sword came from. But anyway, that's not the important part, Herobrine's gone for good and ChuckBone did it," the player said raising his glass. "Here's to ChuckBone!" "To ChuckBone!" the surrounding players repeated holding their glasses in the air and making a toast.

Although he wanted so badly to take off his disguise right now, Herobrine fought the urge. He would have loved to see their expressions change when they realized he was still alive. But that would have to wait, the longer people thought he was dead the better. He had too much on his plate right now trying to find out where the sword came from. The last thing he needed now was another group of players hunting him down.

As Herobrine thought over what the player had said he hoped this was the missing clue he was looking for. Once he found whoever had made the sword he hoped they'd also have the power to create a cure for SparkleGirl. He knew it was a long shot, but he'd nothing else to go on. There was no point in tracking down the witch who had created him, as SparkleGirl had killed her, so that was that plan shot to pieces. Watching the player laugh and joke with his friends, Herobrine hoped this player was the answer to his prayers, for both their sakes. If this was another dead end Herobrine didn't know how he was going to react to that news. SparkleGirl was heading towards her third day with the potion inside her and it was probably getting to a point where she wouldn't be able to turn back. With that thought in mind Herobrine finished off the last of his drink and put his glass on the table. Plan A was taking too long, and it didn't look like this guy was leaving anytime soon. Now it was time for Plan B.

Walking to the table where the group of players were seated, Herobrine singled out the player he was looking for and punched him full in the face knocking him out cold. Then before anyone had a chance to react or say anything, Herobrine threw the limp players body over his shoulder and teleported away. He'd probably blown his cover, but that wasn't most important thing right now.

Find Out What Happens Next In…

AVAILABLE NOW IN ALL ONLINE BOOKSTORES.

## Herobrine Birth Of A Monster Now On Audiobook

Visit iTunes or Audible.com for details.

# Thank You!

A big thank you for buying this copy of ChuckBone - Battle Of The Monstersr. I hoped you enjoyed it. If you did, could you please take a moment now to leave a review? This not only helps me out but it also helps to get this book in front of more readers.

Thanks again.

Barry.

If you like to know more about my books visit www.MinecraftNovels.com or drop by my Facebook page https://www.facebook.com/BarrysMinecraftNovels

Made in the USA
San Bernardino, CA
14 December 2014